BERNICE
and the
Wonder of Pearl

WRITTEN BY

Brandt Ricca

ILLUSTRATED BY

Matt Miller

Ricca, Brandt. *Bernice and the Wonder of Pearl.*

Copyright © 2022 by Brandt Ricca

Illustrations by Matt Miller

Cover layout and book design by Liona Design Co., www.lionadesignco.com

Published by KWE Publishing: www.kwepub.com

ISBN (hardback): 979-8-9853464-9-7
ISBN (paperback): 979-8-9853464-8-0

Library of Congress Control Number: 2022921948

Acknowledgments

Brandt and Matt would like to thank those who have been instrumental in the *Barris Books and Bernice Books* series. Without them, and their belief in dreams and imagination, none of this would be possible.

Their AMAZING manager Kim Eley, Crystal Cregge, Adriane Miller, Brian Winterfeldt and the Winterfeldt IP team, Jonathan Thorpe, The Four Seasons Hotel-Georgetown & The Oxford Exchange.

...and last but not least, all of their friends and family.

Table of Contents

Dedication from the Collaborators

"To the exercise that is getting lost in culture and life, which continues to inspire my stories and imagination."

— BRANDT RICCA, AUTHOR

"To Beverly and Cecilia, whose creative outlooks have influenced my works."

— MATT MILLER, ILLUSTRATOR

1

———

Chapitre Un...

In the big picture of her life she knew this was to be but a moment. But, right there at the start of her summer break, she still wanted to wrap herself in it like her favorite blanket.

She was thinking just that when she felt an arm grab her and pull her back to the sidewalk.

"Dear!" Auntie Taflinda cried. "Stay close to me. New York City is chaotic compared to what you're used to." Bernice and her auntie stood on the corner of a crosswalk in the Big Apple.

A Few Days Before

Bernice Hart was nine years old, and that summer she was spending her school break with her aunties in New York City. Her parents, Mr. and Mrs. Hart, promised her the year prior she could go on the trip as a reward for her being so smart. She skipped a grade at school and was now in her brother Barris' class.

"It's not that I'm smarter than you Barris, I'm just... better!" Bernice would tease her brother whenever he annoyed her. To put it plainly, Barris was not a fan of Bernice's achievements. It felt like an unspoken competition to him.

Oh! I get so wrapped up in telling tales that I forgot to introduce myself. I'm Gracie, and I am a Keeper of the Universe. My job is to monitor the dreams of sleeping children until they are ten years old. I was assigned to Bernice's brother Barris until he crossed the threshold. He is living his pre-teen years now, carrying the lessons taught to him by myself and others. But, like most children around his age, he has started to lose his childish enthusiasm. I'm here to tell you the tale of the children I am assigned to. Now, where was I?

I was with Bernice. And what a delicious treat she was. Her dream worlds were so complex and fun. Bernice knew of her own intelligence, and her teachers were already discussing moving her up another grade. "Barris would love that," Bernice thought.

Bernice was quick as a whip and she was interested in what the world had to offer, unlike her brother and two sisters. Betsy and Betty were teenagers and obsessed with their love lives. Bernice wanted more. And on that trip to New York City, she was going to get it. Three months' worth to be exact.

Mrs. Hart was eager for her youngest child to see that there was more out there, and hoped that Bernice would return with a curious appetite for an ambitious life. As I stood

· ·

in Bernice's bedroom doorway watching Mrs. Hart help pack Bernice's suitcase, you could feel how eager they both were.

As a Keeper, I get to observe the children I've been assigned to, but they can't see me. Nor can I communicate with them. It is only when they slumber that we can chit-chat. But their real lives help me guide them through their childhood and dream universes. I know it all.

"Oh, you'll have a splendid time won't you Bernice? Take it all in and do not leave a single moment unused. That's the worst thing, you know? To leave your life or moments unused." Mrs. Hart folded scarves into Bernice's luggage. "It's so windy between all those skyscrapers, like big wind tunnels, you'll need these scarves for your hair."

"Yes, yes mother. You have told me every single precaution you can think of for New York City," Bernice said impatiently as she peered up from her book, Agatha Christie's *Murder on the Orient Express.* She wasn't helping her mother because she knew her mother would just re-do what she had done.

"Oh, how can you read such dark things, Bernice?" Mrs. Hart said, motioning to Bernice's latest read.

"Because, Mother, Agatha is a brilliant writer and the epitome of a successful woman. When I think of her and her career, well…it naturally makes me start to think of stories that I want to tell and what's possible." Bernice petted her dog Olivier. "Right, Olivier?"

Their mother had learned a ton of French not long ago, to connect with her ancestors, but most of it had faded away by now, aside from calling their dog Olivier, like the French would, with the silent "r," and referring to the family as "mon cheris," and some other random French.

Mrs. Hart stopped mid-fold of a dress. She reached up to touch the pearl necklace she wore and her eyes softened. Sometimes she forgot to think about dreams, imagination, and — most importantly — possibilities.

"Oh, Deerio," Mrs. Hart walked to Bernice. "You are absolutely right. I love you, I love you, I love you, I love you!" Mrs. Hart always said, "I love you" four times to each of her children. "It's because you all are the loves of my life and I want all of you to always remember that and to remember each other."

"What about Dad?" Barris had asked one night, not long ago.

"Well, he is THE love of my life, and he knows that." Mrs. Hart would look at her husband and wink.

"Your mother is my dearest wish," Mr. Hart would respond back.

No matter how cynical one could be, being in the presence of Mr. and Mrs. Hart would make anyone drool over their love for each other and want the same for themselves. Or maybe that's just me when I see them!

Off to the airport the Hart family took Bernice to see her aunties, Mr. Hart's sisters. Bernice bid her family adieu and walked with some sway in her steps to her flight. "So long, New Orleans and dear family!" she cried to her family. "I shall return a big city girl!"

• •

Barris rolled his eyes. "Goodbye, little girl."

Bernice flew on a luxurious Pan Am airplane. Pan Am was THE airline to fly at the time, "Tres la la," Mrs. Hart would say. Bernice flew alone, which felt natural to her as she didn't feel like a child. She was accompanied by a very nice stewardess by the name of Veronica, but she told Bernice to call her "Ronnie." Ronnie had dark brown hair that reached her shoulders, with every strand in perfect place. The hair color matched Bernice's, but not the style. Ronnie's light blue skirt, jacket, and matching hat made a perfect uniform. "Very becoming of you," Bernice said to Ronnie.

"Why, thank you, Bernice! One day when you grow up, maybe you can wear one too. And get one of these." Ronnie pointed to a gold pin she had on her jacket. The Pan Am wings.

Oh! Sitting next to Bernice, flying among the clouds on that spacious airplane, I felt like I was on cloud nine! A gal could get used to this type of life. "Ronnie, some lemonade please," I said. I knew she couldn't hear me, but pretending is fun.

"I can only hope," Bernice said politely. She had bigger plans than riding on planes her whole life. What were they? She didn't know, but she couldn't wait to find out.

In New York City

Auntie Taflinda worked for Coco Chanel, a famous French fashion designer. She lived on the Upper West Side of the city, in a building called The Apthorp. "People who are somebody have lived and live there," Taflinda said as they walked toward the building along the busy summer streets. A big yellow cab had just dropped them off from the airport. Cars honking next to them made the soundtrack to their conversation. Bernice could see waves of heat coming off the tops of all the cars.

Taflinda had lived at The Apthorp for a few years with her sister Sarafina. Sarafina was busy that day at work. She owned a fancy salon, Sarafina's House of Glamour. At her salon, she catered to the bourgeoisie of the city: the people who had money, the people who pretended to have it…and movie stars.

One of those movie stars, Marilyn Monroe, was often in New York City shooting movies. She was a frequent beneficiary of Sarafina's talented hands and scissors.

"She always gives you that extra something you need, ya' know?" Marilyn was overheard whispering to Sarafina's assistant one day. "I will be having the most dreadful day, I come here and I feel like a little piece of me has been glued back together."

The salon was around the corner from where the aunties lived, and Bernice was told that Sarafina would be home later from work. "I was able to take the day off to fetch you today, but most days you will be on your own. Don't worry, our neighbor will be watching you during the day while we work. You'll love her."

Bernice was trying to listen to her auntie but at the same time looking above and around her, taking in New York City and the excitement on display. She found herself giddy, but was doing her best to hold it all in.

• •

"Here we are. Welcome to The Apthorp!" Taflinda said. She turned to Bernice and waved her arm up to point.

Bernice looked at the tall stone archway at the center of the very big building that stood in front of her. It took up multiple blocks. Taflinda guided Bernice through the entrance that led to a courtyard at the center of the apartment complex. In the middle was a circular driveway lined with benches and trees. And in the middle of the driveway was a fountain and flowers and more trees. It was a little oasis. You didn't feel like you were in a city, here in the middle of The Apthorp. I was in awe as I tagged along behind the two.

Once inside the building, Bernice was passing by all sorts of different people. Auntie Taflinda introduced Bernice to each one.

There was Louis Castillo and Dalton Morelock in Apartment 9A, two fellas who lived together and were roommates. Louis was Latin American, with black hair and a stocky build, who smiled with one side of his lip smirking. He was a carpenter. Dalton was an astronaut and had boulders for shoulders, with blonde hair and blue eyes. He had a Southern twang when he talked and was giggly.

Then there was Rosie McGuire and Amelia Hoffman in 10C. Rosie was short, with gray short hair, dressed in high-waisted pants and paint on her clothes. She taught art. Amelia was taller with long black hair, and wore a long skirt and lots of bracelets. She taught music. They were both teachers at the same New York City public school, the Richard Rodgers School of the Arts and Technology.

• •

"Rosie and Amelia are always out to dinners with Louis and Dalton," Taflinda said, narrating the stories of the tenants to Bernice after they'd met. "But they only do that so people don't talk."

Bernice didn't know what her auntie meant by that, and after thinking about it more she still wasn't sure. It was something not many talked about in her world down south—how men sometimes preferred to live with men and women with women.

Taflinda knew the stories of her neighbors from Lonnie the doorman. He delivered the latest gossip to anyone who would listen, often telling his tales while watching the residents of The Apthorp open their own doors.

The aunties lived on the twelfth floor of the building. "To the tip-top we go," Taflinda uttered when she stepped into the elevator with Bernice, holding her luggage beside her.

Bernice had dressed her best to fly that day. "Oh, how marvelous you will be in the air among the clouds," Mrs. Hart had told Bernice when she bought her a new dress to wear for her flight. It was a black dress (Bernice's favorite color) with a white collar and poofed above her knees. It was itchy. Bernice scratched her middle as she and her auntie stood in the elevator. The doors closed and, when they did, they were mirrored. Bernice could see herself, and she liked what she saw. "Golly...what a marvel I am," she thought, staring at her reflection. If anyone thought it was self-confidence Bernice lacked, they were mistaken.

• •

Bernice had dark brown eyes, and dark long brown hair to match. Her hair was thin, but Mrs. Hart had teased it that morning before she pinned it back. "Big trips require big hair," she'd said while she held up the thin strands and combed them aggressively.

The elevator rose slowly up the building and Bernice couldn't wait to see where she would be staying for the summer, her home for adventure. She was thinking about all the things she didn't know would happen and then her thoughts were interrupted by a loud ding.

The twelfth floor.

• •

2

Chapitre Deux...

The aunties' apartment was very big. It was not what Bernice expected for an apartment building. She walked through the white and black marble foyer and stood under an arched doorway, taking it all in.

Large, spacious rooms and tall windows, ornate carved ceilings and crystal chandeliers.

In the corner by the door was a small table that had a stack of different shaped hats on it. Bernice looked to her auntie to explain. "That's your Auntie Sarafina's mess," Taflinda said. "She's been trying a new beehive hairdo. Her hair is like a tall triangle on her head; cockroaches could move in there. She tries on a new hat every day because of the wind, but none will fit. So she throws them on that table." Bernice shrugged her shoulders and continued on the guided tour.

All of the walls had bright white crown molding of different designs. Almost all of the walls were light blue. The "parlor," as Auntie Taflinda called it, was light pink with

thick white curtains that cascaded in layers to the floor. A large fireplace stood on the left side of the parlor.

Two dainty white couches sat in the middle of the room, facing each other. On the glass table in the middle were stacks of *Vogue*, a fashion magazine. "That's the only reading I and your Auntie Sarafina do," Taflinda said.

Bernice felt like she was in too nice a place to even sit. But she did, perching on the edge of one of the white couches.

"Just you and Auntie Sarafina live here?" Bernice asked.

"But of course!" Taflinda answered as she peeled the white elbow-length gloves from her arms and fingers.

"How do you pay for all of this by yourselves?"

"Silly girl, we work. That's what you do when you want to obtain the things you desire. And my biggest desire, you may ask? Well, that's my freedom. Freedom to do what

I want, live where I want, and buy what I want." Taflinda was certain of what she wanted.

"I want freedom too," Bernice replied.

"And you will have it. There is something about you, Miss Bernice. You are already advancing in your studies, you can talk circles around anyone. You ambitious girl, you are going places."

"I'm going to come straight here to live in New York City when I am old enough!" Bernice said excitedly.

Taflinda laughed. "I don't doubt that. So you best get to making friends while you're here. Jamay will show you around the neighborhood."

"Who's Jamay?"

"She's our neighbor. Wonderful young woman, very colorful and just downright fun." Taflinda took the pin out of the light green hat she wore, then undid her blonde bun and shook her hair to let it fall around her shoulders. "She's always such a busy body, I bet grass doesn't get a chance to grow beneath her feet. She's always on the go."

Taflinda was a modern woman of her time. She dressed well, always in chic clothing. She had to: She worked in fashion for Chanel and had to represent the brand well, no matter what she was doing. Pencil skirts with silk ruffled blouses and heels were her signature look.

"Let me show you to your room."

Bernice followed her auntie down a wide hallway, gleaming hardwood floors beneath her feet. White and tan designs in the rugs decorated the hallway floors. On either side of Bernice, on the walls, were photos of the aunties out on the town with friends and on double dates, and large framed French fashion posters. While filigreed sconces glowed along the hallway, it had no windows, and it occurred to Bernice that she could easily lose her way at night in the dark.

Taflinda opened the door at the end of the hall and bright light spilled out. "Voila!"

The room was large, with a queen-sized, fluffy white bed. It was a grown-up bed. "This is just for me?" Bernice asked, her eyes wide. Taflinda nodded.

Bernice thought the bed looked like a giant cloud. A large red oriental rug covered the floor, and the room even had a fireplace. A red plaid chair sat next to the fireplace and stacks of books were on the mantel, on the bedside table, and filling a small bookcase. Bernice was in heaven.

"Jane Austen! Agatha Christie! Virginia Woolf!" Bernice said each author's name with a gasp. "They're all here!"

I must admit, even I was jealous of Bernice's sleeping arrangements. Where I'm from, Norizon, I've never seen a child sleep in such posh style.

"A strong girl needs to read stories from strong women," Taflinda said. "We went to the store and stocked up on some of the greats for you. You can get lost in them when you aren't getting lost in the city." She was excited for Bernice to be there.

"Knock, knock!" Bernice and Taflinda heard a voice.

"That must be Jamay. Come, come!" Taflinda motioned for Bernice to follow her back to the foyer.

"Why, hello there!" Jamay said when they met her in the front of the apartment.

Jamay was a small woman, with a big voice. She had a unique look to her, with almost white blonde hair that went a little below her ears, and bangs that poofed over her eyebrows. She was in her early 20s and was a seamstress, working on costumes for Broadway actors. Her latest job was working on the musical *Carousel*.

She was wearing a knee-length white sleeveless dress with a thin, light yellow belt around her waist. After staring for a bit, Bernice realized Jamay's dress depicted tree branches and different colored birds.

Taflinda had said that Jamay was colorful. And Bernice loved it.

Jamay took both of Bernice's hands in hers. "Ready to get all crazAY in New York CitAY?" she said, her bright smile instantly making Bernice feel happy.

Bernice laughed. "I am."

"I knew you two would hit it off! I have to go change and get back to work," Taflinda said. "Someone's got to make money to pay for you getting crazAY. Be safe!"

"I got her Taf, don't you worry that pristine head of yours," Jamay shouted as Taflinda walked away.

"You know I hate when you call me that," Taflinda said as she closed her bedroom door to change.

• •

"Toodles, Poodles!" she called from her bedroom.

Jamay looked down the hall to see that the coast was clear.

"Alright, kid. You ready?! Let's go!" Jamay grabbed Bernice's hand and they walked out the aunties' front door. "See ya, Taf!"

"Ready for what? Where are we going?"

"It's New York City!" said Jamay. "We can go anywhere."

"What floor do you live on?" Bernice asked.

"I'm on the fifth floor."

"Who do you live with?" Bernice was trying to keep up with Jamay as they walked down the hall. She wasn't used to walking fast. It's a very different way of walking than in New Orleans.

"I live with my husband. He's a jeweler in the Bronx, a family business. His name is Manny, but I call him 'Man.' You know that classic story of a young couple in love? They get married and the young couple's parents buy them a great apartment in the city." Jamay told her story as they walked and it was like she had balls under her feet: She bounced with each step.

While Jamay was tiny, she described her husband Manny as being big in stature. He had enormous muscles and could look intimidating, but he was really very sweet. He ran his family business with a firm hand, but let Jamay run the home life. Manny came from a family that was always teaching him things. His father taught him how to be tough in business and tough on the streets. Manny had a set of brass knuckles that he used as paperweights around his office.

"Because you never know," Jamay said.

Bernice couldn't keep her eyes off of Jamay. She was fascinated by the energy that was pulsating from her. Carefree and confident. She embodied it.

"You know how I knew Manny was for me?" Bernice shrugged her shoulders.

"One day he and his mother were home. This was before we were married. And I went to their house for a date we had planned. It was a fall day. I walked up on the porch to knock on their door. And I paused before I knocked and thought about how much I liked Manny, but didn't know if he liked me." Bernice listened intently. "They had their windows open to let in some cool air. And I overheard Manny talking to his mother. And you know what he had said? He was telling his mother that I was special. That he thought I was like Christmas! Something special that he looked forward to each morning. And well, when a gal hears that, or anyone hears that really, you make that your person."

Bernice's thoughts, let alone her feet, could hardly keep up with Jamay. She liked listening to Jamay, and she loved the halls of The Apthorp! The building was beautiful, with walls of burgundy color, white crown molding, and the same filigreed sconces she'd seen in the aunties' apartment lighting their way.

"This place has a lot of history, ya' know?" Jamay said to Bernice.

• •

"Really?"

"Yep, celebrities live here, people who are making moves in culture, people paving the way. When I saw this building I told my husband that there was no place else for us to be."

Bernice and Jamay stepped into the elevator after hearing the ding signaling its arrival. Down from the twelfth floor they went. The elevator stopped at the ninth floor and opened to the residents who called it home. The doors opened quickly, and there they were…kissing. The couple separated just as quickly as the doors opened.

Bernice's eyes widened. No one moved. The doors shut and the elevator continued its descent.

Bernice stood next to Jamay, speechless.

• •

3

Chapitre Trois...

Jamay hummed happily and moved her shoulders from side to side.

"Did you see that?" asked Bernice.

"See what?"

"Those two men...kissing," Bernice said, trying to fathom what that could mean. She was referring to Louis and Dalton whom she'd met earlier.

"So?" Jamay replied, unfazed.

"Do men kiss each other here in New York?" Bernice asked.

"Oh, you darling little girl," Jamay knelt down to Bernice's eye level as the elevator dinged with each passing floor. "Love is everywhere, even in New York if you can believe it, Bernie. And you should never scoff at love, in the many forms it comes in, with many different people. Love is what everyone wants, and we should admire it when our little pupils see it. Love isn't schlock...ever."

Bernice thought about this. She had never thought of love being in different forms. She had only ever witnessed love on television, in novels, or seen it from her parents. It never dawned on her that love could be between many types of people. Not just a man or a woman. "Love isn't schlock," she repeated in her head.

DING! The elevator doors opened to the lobby. Bernice walked out next to a humming Jamay, who seemed so happy-go-lucky.

"I suppose you're right, Jamay. Love can't be measured or defined. I didn't mean to act as if I knew the definition."

Jamay was impressed by her new friend's outlook. "Oh, it's not a problem, Bernie. You're here for a summer of adventure, right? Well, New York City will deliver that. Now, let's go!"

Bernice didn't know where they were going, nor did she care. She was excited at the prospect of the moments in front of her. Admittedly, I was excited to tag along too — Jamay seemed so fun and spontaneous. I held onto the top of my black beret and bolted out the door of The Apthorp behind them.

As they walked down Broadway, Jamay twirled in front of Bernice so her flowing dress would dance in the breeze. As she twirled, Jamay lifted her arms wide, embracing the breeze, embracing New York. Something about her was magical. Bernice was enamored by her free spirit. She *did* seem like Christmas.

"Bern, we gotta go to my job for a quick minute so I can grab my paycheck," Jamay said while she hurried Bernice

along. "I have to buy Manny a gift for his birthday."

"Where do you work?" Bernice inquired.

"Why, on Broadway!" Jamay exclaimed and did a high skip in the air. "Where dreams are born, where dreams are lived, and where dreams sometimes die. I'm working on a show called *Carousel*. It's great! It's only going to run through August. I love all the cast and crew I work with. Especially Jo, she's the main gal, and an amazing actress and singer. I could watch her all day."

As for Bernice, she couldn't take her eyes off Jamay, and listened with all her attention. She didn't want to miss a word Jamay had to say amidst the busy sidewalks of the city.

"My show is by Rodgers and Hammerstein, ya' know. They're a big, big, BIG theater-writing team. I just absolutely adore their work. I find myself singing along to songs from their shows while I work on costumes. This morning while doing dishes, thinking about meeting you today, I found myself singing, *'Getting to know you, getting to know all about you. Getting to like you, getting to hope you like me.'"*

Jamay paused to look at Bernice, to see if she could find recognition on her face. A pedestrian walked past and applauded Jamay's little tune. Jamay curtsied.

It was partly cloudy that day in New York City but the clouds parted for a brief moment and it was as if Jamay had her own spotlight from the sun among all the fast-walking people.

Bernice nodded her head trying to show she recognized the song, but it was obvious she didn't know it. "Oh, c'mon Bernie! You don't know *The King and I?!* Ohhhh, it's about forbidden love, freedom, overcoming prejudices. It has everything one experiences in one's life."

After a hop, a skip, and a buck-fifty cab ride, Bernice and Jamay had landed themselves at the theater inside City Center on West 55th Street. It was a tall stone building, with half a circle engraved on the front of it. Bernice thought it reminded her of a church.

Jamay took her to the side entrance that had "STAGE DOOR" written in big black letters on it. "You need to stay right here, okay Bernice?" Bernice could tell Jamay was being serious from using her full name. "I need to quickly grab my paycheck and I'll be right out. They're working on the set today and it's no place for a young girl to be running around. But don't move. I'll be swift."

Jamay swung open the metal door wide enough that Bernice could catch a glimpse inside. I was curious myself and stood behind Bernice, craning my head to look. I was standing so close to her that I think Bernice felt my breath on the back of her neck. And that's odd. Normally, my assigned children have no idea of my presence when they are awake and I am observing.

As the door slowly swung shut, we both saw the stage, a big spotlight shining down on the middle. Crew members were carrying wood, ropes, and paint, but they appeared to be shadows because of the spotlight. A busy shadow scene. It seemed exciting and romantic. The sound of instruments being tuned echoed.

Bernice immediately wondered how to keep from

getting bored with herself on a side street, no book to keep her company. She looked up to the rectangle of sky she could see, with all the buildings around her. She began to miss nature a little bit, and thought of running in a field with her favorite book, snatching up some honeysuckle as an afternoon treat. Just as she got lost in the taste of honey, she was startled by Jamay's voice.

"Lordy Pajordy! That took longer than expected." Jamay tucked an envelope of money into her purse.

Jamay and Bernice then spent the afternoon sampling ice cream from a street vendor and walking in Central Park, which Bernice thought was the biggest park she had ever seen. She was sure it was the biggest in the whole world. Jamay took her to Times Square, where the chaos nearly overwhelmed Bernice.

"I think we can head back now," Bernice told Jamay.

"Ya' sure, Bernie? I can take ya' around a bit more."

"I'm sure. We have three whole months. We can take our time covering the land of New York."

At that moment, Bernice felt like she was an adult, watching Jamay.

Bernice and Jamay walked under the archway of The Apthorp and Bernice felt the relief of being "home" after walking around all day with Jamay.

"Your aunties should be home from work by now," Jamay said as they left the elevator on the twelfth floor. Jamay walked Bernice to the apartment door.

• •

"And this, my newest gal pal, is where I bid you adieu. BUT, I shall see you tomorrow." Jamay grabbed Bernice's hand and gave it a kiss. Bernice felt awkward at the affection from someone she hardly knew.

"Bye." Bernice abruptly walked into her aunties' apartment and closed the door.

"Bernice, is that you darling? We picked up Chinese for dinner," Auntie Sarafina shouted from down the hall.

Bernice looked at Sarafina's pile of hats at the door, smelled the delicious take-out, and walked toward the kitchen, her mouth watering.

4

Chapitre Quatre

In her aunties' apartment was an open kitchen with a small, round table under a window and four chairs.

Sarafina was standing at the unlit stove, which looked as if it had never been used. She had taken off her heels and had one foot stacked on the other, stockings still on. She was leaning over a box of Chinese food, dropping noodles down her throat with her fingers.

"Bernice!" Sarafina exclaimed, her mouth still full of noodles. She ran to Bernice, wiping her hands on a napkin, and gave her a warm hug.

Sarafina was a short woman. She wore wedges every day, and would explain that they were more comfortable since she was on her feet all day cutting and styling hair. She was quite accomplished as a stylist and owned her own salon. As if to make up for her height, she styled her black hair into a very tall hairdo. Taflinda was right, saying cockroaches could move in. Bernice thought her hair looked like the mud crawfish holes she and her siblings spotted in New Orleans in the summer. Sarafina always wore a high-waisted pencil skirt and a short-sleeved collared blouse. She had highly defined dark eyebrows arching above her eyes.

"Oh, Lovey, I'm so excited for you to be here for the summer, we'll have such fun!" From the record player came the voice of Judy Garland, the woman who played Dorothy as a little girl in the *Wizard of Oz.*

"Have you seen this film?" Sarafina asked Bernice, motioning to the record player. *Summer Stock* with Judy Garland and Gene Kelly. "Oh, it's my favorite. These are all the songs from it. Always puts one in a good mood after a long day."

"If you feel like singing, sing. Tra la la your cares away..." Sarafina sang along.

"Where's Auntie Taflinda?" Bernice asked.

"Why, I am right here," Taflinda said, walking into the kitchen. "And I am famished."

Bernice was not used to such a relaxed dinner atmosphere. It was a far cry from the dinner table at the Hart residence in New Orleans.

• •

At that moment, Bernice felt a little homesick. She missed the routine of hearing her mother's ramblings and everyone gathering at the table.

Bernice snapped herself out of the feeling. One thing Bernice had always done was to let herself feel her inner emotions, process them even if just for a moment, and then release them. Bernice believed this routine let her feel what she needed to feel, but then move on and not let it rule her day.

"How was your day with Jamay?" Taflinda asked her niece.

"It was great! She's really fun and interesting. We had a great first day in the city. Times Square is a lot!" Bernice said.

"Oh, only tourists go there, my sweet," Sarafina said, gobbling noodles. "If you live here, you don't ever go near there unless you are going to the theater."

"We were there for Jamay to grab her paycheck," Bernice explained.

"Now *that* is a girl you should definitely take notes from, Bernice," Taflinda said as she helped herself to noodles from the box. "While you're here I don't want you being an old shoe. Do you want some noodles? We get them from Mr. Lee's. Sooo good." Taflinda hopped onto the kitchen counter to eat and gestured for Bernice to join her and Sarafina at the stove. Bernice was taken aback at how casual they were in the kitchen.

"An old shoe?" Bernice asked, helping herself to the box.

"Yep, an old shoe…too comfortable," Taflinda responded. "Step out of your comfort, explore, be inspired…and do it on purpose."

"That's the plan," Bernice said, between mouthfuls of noodles. "I shall thoroughly explore the city. But also read when not exploring. I can't wait to dive into those books in my bedroom."

"That's right, Bernice. Explore and read." Sarafina had stooped to pick up her shoes and was holding them over her shoulder. "I have always found that people who read just know more about everything. I like to only read my *Vogue* magazine, BUT, I know a bit more than the person who reads nothing." Sarafina blew a kiss to Bernice and walked out of the kitchen. "Toodles poodles! I'm off to bed. My tootsies need to rest."

Everyone in Bernice's family called feet their tootsies.

Taflinda looked at Bernice. "We don't have any strict rules here—a very casual home life. Go to bed when you're tired and eat when you're hungry. The only thing we ask is that you contribute. Contribute to yourself while staying here and try each day on for size. See what fits."

Bernice thought that sounded exciting and fun— if a little scary. She'd had constant butterflies in her stomach since she'd arrived just a few hours before. She felt as if she had grown a few years already. Being around all these strong women. And it was only Tuesday!

Taflinda packed away the Chinese and put it in the yellow refrigerator. "Now, off to bed you go. You have some more exploring to do with Jamay tomorrow."

Bernice stood and hugged her auntie goodnight.

She left Taflinda in the kitchen and walked down the hall to brush her teeth. It had been a busy day and she suddenly realized she was tired.

Staring at her reflection in the bathroom mirror, Bernice said to herself, "I'm brushing my teeth in New York City." It felt so fancy. She closed the door of her New York City bedroom. "Now I'm in my New York City bedroom." It was fun to remind herself of it.

She slipped on her pajamas, a flowy white, short-sleeved top with ruffles on the collar and hem and matching white pants. Mrs. Hart had packed them for Bernice, who acted as if she hated them in front of her mother. But secretly, they made her feel like a pretty girl, and she loved that.

She crawled into her big grown-up bed, fluffy like a marshmallow. The sheets were crisp and cool, which was nice after being outside on a hot summer day. She grabbed her Agatha Christie book to continue the tale of *Murder on the Orient Express.*

Bernice started to read the words of the character Monsieur Bouc, who was the sidekick of the investigator in the novel. "All around us are people, of all classes, of all nationalities, of all ages..." Before long, her eyelids grew heavy and closed. The book tipped back onto the bed and she was asleep.

Now remember, as I've told you before, each child enters their dream universe based on their surroundings when they start to slumber. Barris, Bernice's brother, would ride away on musical notes from Frenchman Street in New Orleans.

Bernice was always surrounded by books and words.

• •

Each night she would drift away on the words from her favorite books. Excerpts from the stories would swarm the walls of her room:

"By name I know not how to tell thee who I am," from *Romeo and Juliet* by Shakespeare.

"And they were both ever sensible of the warmest gratitude," from *Pride and Prejudice* by Jane Austen.

"Mrs. Dalloway said she would buy the mangonel flowers herself," from *Mrs. Dalloway* by Virginia Woolf.

All lines and words from pages of books Bernice had read.

Her dream universe was the same in New York City as it was at her house in New Orleans. After a moment, her bedroom wall was covered with words and then they poured onto Bernice as if bursting from the top of a waterfall.

The words gently gathered her up and carried her out the window.

Bernice opened her eyes mid-flight and all she saw were words. Then, all was black.

The words from stories and books she loved set her on solid ground. Bernice lost her bearings for a moment but then she heard a familiar tune.

It was "Clair de Lune." It was a song she had learned to play on the piano a year prior, a piece that she had performed when the aunties had visited New Orleans.

All around her was black, until a figure in the corner of her eye caught her attention. All the while, the tune slowly danced around her.

• •

5

Chapitre Cinq...

Bernice turned to see…a bird woman? She had dark skin, red feathers for a skirt, with the same feathers decorating her arms up to her shoulders. The red feathers shimmered in the light. She had black hair piled high, as if three bowls sat on top of her head. The woman—for it was a woman, not a bird—was standing at a big square silver microphone. She was moving in slow motion underneath a spotlight, pushing out her arm holding the mic, then pulling it closer to her while she sang. Red feathers fell slowly behind her.

Bernice didn't hear any words coming out of the woman's mouth. The only sound was a piano playing "Clair de Lune."

A lightning bug moved past Bernice's ear in the darkness, then landed on her nose. The piano music stopped. Bernice contemplated the firefly on her nose, but just for a moment. It exploded into hundreds and then thousands of little fireflies that flickered in front of her face.

The woman had disappeared.

The fireflies continued multiplying and were now forming lines, then more lines, and the lines started taking the shape of paths, structures, and objects. A fountain sprang up with a statue in the center of it.

A world of light was forming before Bernice's eyes.

Lights glowed in little puddles of water. It looked as if white fireworks were going off under the surface.

The clusters of lightning bugs that had formed Bernice's dream world started to fade away, objects took on color and the land was complete.

Bernice stood in awe.

I flew in to greet her. That's right, I can fly now! I am older than when I was with Barris and had developed advanced abilities. As we Keepers age and we are assigned more children to help, we get older physically, but mentally we still have our childish enthusiasm intact. It helps us when we're guiding each child through their dream worlds. And more importantly, our belief remains that anything is possible.

I bounced off some of the remaining fireflies and landed right in front of Bernice.

"Ahoy there! I am at your service madam!" I spun around quickly to twirl my big brown coat and flicked off some firefly dust. My long red spaghetti hair tossed in the breeze under my black beret.

Bernice was startled and jumped back. The ruffles of her white pajama shirt fluttered in the air.

"Who are you?!" Bernice asked me. I was having déjà vu from her brother Barris asking me the same question a while back, when I first met him in Rappa.

"I am Gracie! I am your Keeper. I was your brother's, too. It is my job to help you navigate your dream worlds when there is a problem. And we figure it out together."

"Where did you come from?"

"Norizon, of course. Dream headquarters, where we monitor all the dreams of sleeping children around the world. And this is only one of your dream worlds, Bernice. Welcome to Perna!"

Bernice looked around her at the now visible world and fading firefly dust. An orange shimmer continually waved through the world, as if driven by gusts of wind. Bernice looked up to a black, starlit sky. She felt so small. The stars vibrated with a glow. A barely perceptible crack in the sky seemed to glow too. It looked out of place.

A tune started to play from the fountain in the center of Perna. And as it played, emerald green fields formed around the puddles of glowing water. From the emerald fields, large trees sprang up with glowing moss dangling from them. Then little floating wooden houses appeared; they were four foot squares, with little smoking chimneys. The houses floated through the grass, as if the grass had the consistency of water. The water itself was solid. Bernice realized she was standing on water and could walk on the surface.

While observing Bernice take in her dream world of Perna, I bent down and splashed some of the grass on her.

"Hey!" Bernice shouted.

"You can't just stare at your dreams, Bernice, you have to grab them! We are in one right now." I splashed more grass on her. Green sparkles dripped from her pajamas.

Bernice exhaled a small laugh, starting to relax.

"You said there is a problem here. What is it?" she asked.

"That I don't know. The bulb on our Dream Sani (SAN-nye) went from red to pale yellow."

"What's a Dream Sani?"

"It's a big board in Norizon where all of the children's dream worlds are shown in lightbulbs. They are all different colors. When the color changes and doesn't stay consistent, it means there is something wrong. Then a Keeper is assigned to that child, and we come down to help explore and solve."

As Bernice and I stood on the water, we were shaken by a dreamquake—like an earthquake but in a dream. It was such a big shake that Bernice fell into a puddle of grass with emerald glitter splashing up. I had to pick her up quickly, and used some of my power to exude air from my hand to help dry her off.

Bernice was impressed, watching me. "I want to have that magic."

We heard a cracking sound and then the glowing crack in the sky opened further above us. The little floating houses were bumping against each other from the dreamquake. Waves of grass splashed up the sides of the fountain. The glowing moss dangling from the trees waved and had become brighter, as if inflamed.

Bernice glared at me with a wondering expression.

"I guess we see what the problem is," I said.

The fountain, made of dark stone, had a large statue of a woman in the center. She looked very grand. Bright water splashed around her, creating a constant luminous mist. The dress the statue wore flared out and created the mist that was floating in the air. It was so bright around the fountain that it was hard to see at first, but I noticed a small open window at the base.

"Let's go in there," I told Bernice. "I think I hear something."

"I don't hear anything," she said. She came closer and listened intently. "What is that?"

We both heard humming from the window.

"Mmhum, Uhmhum, mmhummmm."

"It's singing!" Bernice shouted, excited at the fact she DID hear it.

"Let's go!" I grabbed Bernice's hand and we ran toward the fountain. My instincts told me we could jump right into the open window.

I leaped up and pulled Bernice with me. Mid-air, Bernice saw a plaque above the statue.

"The Wonder of Pearl" it read. Bernice silently repeated it. *"The Wonder of Pearl."*

And then she realized it.

"It's the woman I saw!" thought Bernice, recognizing the statue as the woman in red feathers she'd seen earlier, silently singing. And at that moment, as Bernice and I dove through the window, a woman's laugh echoed into the distance.

• •

6

Chapitre Six

As Bernice and I landed on the other side of the window, Bernice felt goosebumps. She could still hear the woman's laughter echoing behind us.

"You okay?" I asked her.

"I am just...swell." Bernice patted the ruffles on her pajamas as a reflex to feel like she had some sort of control.

Music filled our ears, along with the sound of a crowd.

Bernice and I both turned away from the dark window we had just come through to a spectacle.

We were in a large, circular, wood-paneled room, where every other panel was lit from behind with a bright white light. It was like we were on the inside of a striped lampshade.

Above us were sparkling gold rafters with tables full of people below, laughing and enjoying themselves. On the rafters above them were also people sitting with their feet dangling, while others walked from one to the other. The people were all different colors: yellow, brown, black, white, blue. Men had their arms around each other, women were doing the same. Groups of others sat in mixed company, all enjoying each other's laughter. Each was dressed in dapper clothing, and they all had gold glitter on their skin, their clothes, and hair, glitter floating around each one.

Music was playing from a golden stage in the back of the room. Above it were dangling shimmering pieces of paper.

From a loudspeaker somewhere in the room came a booming voice. "I now present to you, Fefe and the Fefettes!"

A Black man wearing a hat began to play a piano on stage, the fingers of his left and right hands going back and forth quickly on the keys. The piano notes quieted the room, but only for a moment.

Suddenly, loud applause and cheering as a swirl of purple feathers began to fall from above the stage. Little tornadoes of swirling purple feathers spun toward the floor and out of the commotion rose two hands and arms, then a young woman's head. Fefe. She wore elbow-length white gloves, and she stood posing as the audience cheered. The purple feathers stopped swirling, becoming her dress.

• •

Three swirls of gold feathers began to form and spin behind her. They grew taller and formed a man and two women, the Fefettes, dressed in their gold-feathered best: a tuxedo and two gowns.

The crowd became silent, the piano man ceased playing, and Fefe began to sing.

First, she belted out a single note. *"Ohhhhhh..."* The audience held their collective breath. Then she hummed the note and started to sway side to side. The three Fefettes behind her started to do the same, snapping their fingers. The rhythm was easy and slow.

She swayed in the spotlight.

The pace picked up as Fefe made eye contact with the piano man and he resumed playing. Along with her singing, and the Fefettes accompanying her vocals behind her, musicians playing horns started to rise from the floor behind them. The lights in the crowd went low, and the lights on the platform with Fefe became brighter.

Bernice felt the glow from the stage and was starstruck.

I must admit I was captivated too, along with the crowd.

When Fefe neared the end of her tune, the crowd was clapping and singing. Then she stopped, signaling for everyone to stop too.

Bernice was so enthralled that she was still clapping. I had to grab her hands for her to stop.

Fefe finished the song a cappella, with no instruments playing.

After she sang each line, the Fefettes repeated it.

The spotlight went off, the Fefettes' voices echoed, and the room was dark but for a moment. Then the lights came back on, with Fefe gone from the stage. The people all stood to applaud and cheer.

"Where did she go?" Bernice asked me.

"I'm not sure. I would love to congratulate her on her performance."

"There!" Bernice pointed across the room to a corner.

I looked just in time to see the purple feather train on Fefe's dress slide out through an opening.

"Let's go tell her how spectacular she was." I grabbed Bernice to run toward the corner. But when we got there, we saw no door or opening. "But this is where she was! She went through here." Bernice looked crushed. I was disappointed too.

"She had to get out of here somehow," I said. I pushed my shoulder against the corner and a hidden door appeared in the wall. We walked through and left the excitement of the room behind us.

Now we were among a forest of weeping willow trees. They all swayed back and forth with glowing leaves and moss hanging from the branches. The stars above were glowing too, brighter and then dimmer.

One of the willows was moving more than the others, swaying dramatically but in slow motion.

"Look!" Bernice pointed to a trail of purple feathers.

(Bernice was a very observant girl.) The feathers all floated just above the grassy ground, like a trail of purple breadcrumbs leading to the slowly waving willow tree.

"Well," Bernice said. We looked at each other. "What are we waiting for?"

One thing we had forgotten was that we could walk on water in this world, and grass was like puddles. We both started to run on a grassy trail. It splashed up green glitter as we ran to the swaying willow.

We laughed, admiring the sparkles splashing up around us. They froze mid-air for a second and then floated slowly back onto the grass. We could still hear the sound of piano keys behind us, but it was becoming more and more distant.

As we approached the glowing, swaying moss in the tree, Bernice and I both stopped.

"Is that gonna shock us?" Bernice asked.

"I'll test it out." I knew that I could bounce back more quickly than Bernice due to my Keeper abilities.

I reached out to touch the moss and as I did, "Ahhh!" Bernice had hit my arm to scare me.

"BERNICE!" I shouted, jumping back. "You are just like your brother."

"That is the meanest thing you have ever said to me," Bernice replied.

I tried again to touch the hanging moss. When I did, sticky gold dust came off and stained my hand. I had to wipe my hands on my big brown coat to clean them.

• •

"Ick!" Bernice exclaimed.

"It's safe to touch and to go inside, that's what's important."

We both pushed through the moss. Bernice rolled her pajama sleeves up so as to not get gold dust on them.

When we arrived inside the tree, a glowing umbrella of light extended over us. We saw no one and nothing but the middle of the tree.

"Fefe has quite the little disappearing act," Bernice said.

I stood in silence and closed my eyes.

"What are you doing?' Bernice asked.

"Shush girl, I need to concentrate."

I kept my eyes closed to see the back of my eyelids. I had developed a new ability recently. When I closed my eyes and concentrated, it was as if a movie projector would project from my pupils and play on the screen that was the back of my eyelids. I could view what I was seeking.

What started to play on the back of my eyes was this:

Purple feathers floating in the air where Bernice and I stood at that moment. A glowing crack in a jagged line shining brighter than the moss that lit up the inside of the tree. A white gloved hand smoothed the crack to appear straight again. Then the hand was gone.

I opened my eyes and looked to the corner where I'd "seen" that straight line. If you stared at it for a little bit, you could see it was brighter than the rest of the glowing atmosphere.

• •

"What is it?" Bernice wanted to know.

"There's a crack in this world," I said. "And it appears our talented Miss Fefe has left through it."

Bernice then heard the same echoing laugh again. She rubbed her arms. Goosebumps.

• •

7

Chapitre Sept...

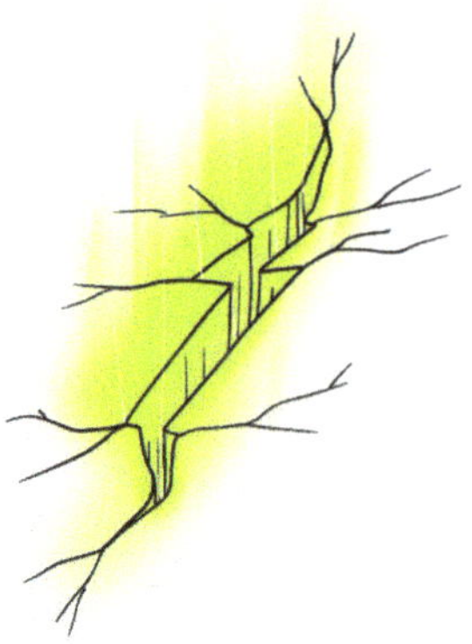

"D o you hear that?" Bernice asked me.

"Hear what?" I hadn't heard anything. My focus was on the barely visible crack in the tree where Fefe's dress of purple feathers had disappeared. "Let's go in and get Fefe."

The ground started to shake again, and with the shaking, the glowing moss gave off clouds of gold dust.

"We should hurry and get this sorted out." I pushed against the crack, my senses telling me that Fefe had the answers.

The crack became wider, and as it opened, a bright green light blasted through. "Grab my hand and don't let go," I told Bernice.

I felt her fingers intertwined with mine and I covered my eyes with my free hand.

I could sense that the light had dimmed and it was safe to open my eyes once we passed through the crack. I heard it close behind us like a heavy metal door.

When I opened my eyes I saw Bernice just staring. I found myself turning around and then doing the same.

The sky was filled with waves of lights of green and silver, moving like curtains up above, like the aurora borealis in the Northern Hemisphere. The waves lit up the entire space in front of us.

We heard locusts. All around us were floating particles of shimmering gold glitter and a ground that was layered with something sparkling and white, like snow. Straight down the center of this foreign sight were chimneys of shiny brick that were the size of an adult person. Too many to count. They each had a glow coming out of the top.

At each chimney top stood a short, chubby little person. You couldn't see their faces. Pointed hats covered their eyes, and they all held large sticks that were taller than them. They wore dark green pants, oversized white tops, and yellow shoes that curled on the end. They reminded me of what elves must have been like at the North Pole.

"What is this place?" Bernice looked at me.

"I'm not sure. I've heard of places like this within a child's dream universe, but I have never seen it myself. I think this is your dream depot, Bernice."

"What's a dream depot?"

"A dream depot is where the entrances to all the dream worlds reside in each child's dream universe. You can have countless dream worlds, or some children only have a few if their imagination dwindles. Your imagination could take the form of hope or of optimism. Rarely are you able to access the depot because it is protected by guards, which are the people you see before you." I pointed to rows of guards standing silently at each chimney top. "They're supposed to protect the entrance to each dream world within your mind. We Keepers enter your dream worlds another way, from dream headquarters in Norizon."

"Hey! Let me through!" My dream lesson to Bernice was interrupted by Fefe screaming to one of the guards of dreams.

"Look, there she is!" Bernice shouted and started running toward her. I ran after her.

"Fefe! Oh my gosh, I am such a fan! We tried to talk to you after the show, but you disappeared," Bernice said, almost tumbling over her words from how quickly she was talking.

I was almost embarrassed by how eager Bernice was acting.

"Who are you, child?" Fefe asked, her purple-feathered dress draped all around her.

"Ahoy there! I'm Gracie and this is Bernice. We were trying to compliment your performance but we were interrupted by some quakes and rumbles. And we kinda sorta followed you here."

"Oh," Fefe said, seeming to be more calm now. "Well you shouldn't follow me. I don't need any company where I am going."

"Where are you going?" Bernice asked.

"Anywhere but here," Fefe said, sternly.

"But aren't you supposed to perform every night? Why do you want to leave? And why is there a crack in the dream world?" I had many questions.

"Please step aside," the guard said to us. "You do not have the authority to enter." The guard spoke in a whisper, and we didn't see his lips move when he spoke.

"Yes, you have told me many times. Girls, let's go over there." Fefe pointed to a patch of green nearby, and she shot the guard an angry look.

The green patch wasn't grass, more like layers of plush blankets piled together. We sat on top of them while the sky continued its green and silver light show. Around us were items you'd find in an attic—an old lamp. A trunk. An unhinged door.

"It all started with Pearl," Fefe began.

"Pearl the statue?" Bernice asked.

"Yes dear, she is a statue."

"I think I saw her when I first got here."

Fefe, who was looking up at the sky, looked quickly to Bernice. "You saw Pearl when you got here?"

• •

"Yeah, she was singing in slow motion and then she disappeared. I think I have been hearing her laugh too."

"You didn't tell me that," I said to Bernice.

"I wasn't sure what it was, and that's why I didn't say anything."

"Pearl was THE girl of this world. Many many nights ago, our world was in chaos. Lots of confusion. Our people were seeking to leave. And then Pearl stood outside amongst the fireflies and started to sing. And oh, could she sing! Everyone stopped in their tracks to listen. After a while, we all forgot about the uncertainty of our world and every night we went to hear her sing. It was what we all looked forward to. And as long as Pearl sang, all was well."

"Did Pearl sing where we saw you singing earlier tonight?' I asked her.

"Yep, it has always been there. And when Pearl moved on, on to wherever legends go, this world erupted that statue of her as an extension of its gratitude for her service, her talent, and her compassion."

"Wow." Bernice looked off into the distance at the row of chimneys and their dedicated guards.

"When I was younger," Fefe continued, "I remember one night I saw Pearl performing, and I thought at that moment she had achieved everything I thought dreams were made of. She seemed happy, successful, and desired. And it was then...that I met Grelda."

Of course, Grelda was the dream universe witch

· ·

of all sleeping children. And she tends to have her hand in everything, as pesky as that may be, and sometimes her spells are a little sloppy because she is so busy. But in the end, her spells are always for a reason.

Grelda also teaches all Keepers in Norizon at a school, on how to navigate dreams.

"You struck a deal with Grelda?" I asked. Bernice looked confused, so I explained who Grelda was.

"That I did," said Fefe. "It seemed so right at the time. After Pearl transitioned into Kenos, her next phase where she'd be immortalized, Grelda put a spell on me that I would be the one to take over for Pearl. I would have all that Pearl had as long as I stayed in this dream world and sang every night."

As Fefe spoke, I remembered the Clown of Trell transitioning to that phase when I was there with Barris, the phase when someone is ready to move to the next level of their life. Whether it be still with us, or not, but it's their time.

"Oh, Dearie," I said as I thought of that story.

"But after I sang one night, I went to the glowing willow and sat there and dreamed about everything else I wanted to do...at least to explore doing. As I lay inside the tree and looked up, a flower bloomed next to me with thin, white, feather petals. I picked it up and wished to dream more and to be more. The instant I blew those feathers off the stem, they swirled around me and then I heard a crack."

I looked back to the crack that was visible not far behind us, still glowing in the distance.

· ·

Fefe sighed. "Now I come here trying to peek inside those chimneys over there. And I was able to one night because the guard had fallen asleep. And gee, what I saw inside! A whole other world of possibilities. But since then I can't get in. Obsession has taken over and I lose track of time and will miss my performance sometimes."

"And that is why the world shakes. You don't perform EVERY night anymore," Bernice said, putting together the puzzle pieces.

"Right on the nose, Bernice," Fefe said. She sighed again and looked up, humming a tune that sounded similar to the song we'd heard her sing minutes before. As she hummed, her Fefettes appeared out of nowhere, humming behind her in harmony.

"What the…?!" I asked Fefe.

Fefe looked behind her. "Oh, them? They go everywhere with me."

8

Chapitre Huit...

We sat listening to Fefe and the Fefettes hum together. Bernice and I were still digesting what we'd just heard. What was Grelda thinking, casting such a spell on Fefe and limiting her dreams forever?

"Well, we need to fix this problem," I said. "You can't go on and perform every night. It'd be one thing if you were happy, but one person can't do the same thing over and over again, especially if they aren't happy! And those people who come and see you, they have to want something too, something else for themselves."

Bernice jumped up, startling the Fefettes.

"What's wrong?" I asked.

"There! Do you hear it?" Bernice looked all around her. It was the same laugh she'd heard ever since she arrived in her dream world.

"I hear her too." Fefe said calmly. I didn't hear anything.

• •

We were in the dream depot so we didn't feel the rumble, but we heard it. Off in the distance, the world of Perna, where we had snuck out the backdoor, was shaking. Firefly dust was billowing up. In that moment, the fear of the unknown made me wish my grandmother Lucy was with me to help solve this case. She was a great Keeper, and always had great intuition. She had become lost in a little girl's dream world not long ago. And a name that is burned in my memory popped into my head…Eloise.

Flashback to Norizon, Dream Headquarters

"Gracie, did you hear what I said?" Lucy looked down at her granddaughter. "And did what I say matter?" She grabbed Gracie's chin so their eyes met.

They were sitting on the main floor of Norizon, which was abuzz with Keepers running here and there, carrying folders with details of their cases. It was like a busy 1920s Hollywood hotel: burgundy walls, gold accents, gleaming lights. In the middle was Helfi, the concierge for the dream headquarters, who monitored the dream board of all the children's dream worlds. He would hand out case folders each day to Keepers.

"This little boy is going through trouble at home. This little girl's best friend moved away. These siblings have a sick mother." He would be reading the folders as he handed them out, occasionally looking up at the Keepers. He spotted Lucy.

"Lucy!" Helfi shouted from his center station, "I have a new one for you; it's a doozie."

Lucy walked past the band of floating instruments that provided the background music for Norizon. She took the case folder from Helfi.

"Little girl named Eloise. Having a rough go of it lately. She's recently lost a good friend and is having friction with her mum. Good luck with this one, Lovey. I'm sensing some storms with her."

Lucy read the case file for a moment and then looked up. "Gracie, let's go to the room. I need to do some last minute training."

They walked, hand in hand, to the white square — the Kystra (KIS-stra) — and four walls slid up from the gold trim and closed over them to lift them past the different floors of Norizon.

"Where are we going, Grandma?" Young Gracie tugged on her grandmother's big brown coat.

"To the Larix. We have to meet Neo for some research." She patted Gracie's black beret.

The four walls slid back down, exposing the two to a padded training area where Lucy's longtime friend Neo sat with his back to the Kystra. The back of his long ponytail glimmered down his orange trench coat. All Keepers wear long trench coats that carry all their supplies while they move about the dreams of children. Neo turned. The first thing Gracie remembered about Neo was the deepest purple of his eyes. All Keepers have purple eyes, the color of wisdom (of dreams), devotion (to their assigned child), and of course...of magic.

Neo and Lucy grew up together and were Keepers in training the same year. Many nights before, Neo's father, Nevarre, had become lost in a little boy's dream world and had not been heard from since. A Keeper becomes lost when they encounter a child who has broken dreams. Nevarre was a great Keeper, and in his absence Neo had made it his mission to improve a Keeper's job, knowledge, and to find how to rescue those who are lost. Some would say he was obsessed.

Lucy was determined to never become lost herself, and consulted frequently with Neo when she knew broken dreams were a possibility.

In the Larix with all the different colored pillows and padding, Keepers could practice their mobile abilities: flying, teleporting from one space to another, flipping off walls, extending their arms and legs, and more. These abilities helped prepare them for any type of dream.

Gracie loved watching her grandmother and Neo's disciplined practice. She hoped she would be able to rise to their level.

After a few hours of working on physicality with Neo, where they flew, leaped and stretched their limbs as far as they could go as if they were putty, they moved to the Storik (STOR-rik), where the history of Keepers and dreams were kept and where Neo spent most of his time. If a Keeper finds themself in a broken dream, it becomes a stormy labyrinth and the Keeper can get disconnected from their assigned child, which keeps them lost. Keeping up with any type of mobile skills and honing new ones is key.

Amongst the stacks of books, banker lamps, and piles of papers in the Storik, Lucy and Gracie listened to Neo talk about how dreams become broken and the children who suffer them.

"A broken dream is born of a broken heart. The child has been through something horrible or is experiencing unpleasant circumstances. Their dream worlds are full of storms, winds, and the things that can cause a Keeper to become lost. Separation from their Keeper begins the dwindling of a child's enthusiasm."

Gracie looked up to her grandmother, feeling scared.

Neo continued. "When a Keeper becomes separated from their child, they aren't with them to help them navigate their troubles. The child doesn't dream for much longer after that. There is a slumber of nothingness."

Lucy walked to the marble table, which was next to file cabinets stacked against the walls as high as the eye could see. On the table were piles of books and papers. Lucy pointed to the open book that had Nevarre's name and his story on it.

"A Keeper is not with their child when they wake up from a broken dream, when we could normally observe them, which helps us guide them when they sleep," Neo continued. "The Keeper is stuck in that dream world. Lost in a labyrinth of unpleasant things."

• •

Gracie looked down at the book with Nevarre's story. "Geez. Can a Keeper be rescued?"

"Not before now, but that's what we are working on here."

Just then, a tall woman came out of the shadows into the room. She wore a tan trench coat with a gold belt around her waist. Her purple eyes picked up glints of the glowing hair that surrounded her head like a halo.

"Who is she?" Gracie asked.

"That's Simone," Neo said. "She's a Keeper who is not as well known here in Norizon, as she doesn't trumpet her successes like some other Keepers do. But she has helped many children. She's a silent treasure among us Keepers." Neo smiled kindly at Simone as she approached the table.

"But she has all of the powers a Keeper can have," he continued. "And more importantly, she's here to help us rescue lost Keepers and to piece back together broken dreams. Gracie, meet Simone."

"Absolutely my pleasure to meet you, little one," Simone curtsied to Gracie, trying to make her feel welcome. Gracie curtsied back. "I like to keep a low profile. Can't let everyone always know what we're up to now, can we?" She winked at Gracie.

Gracie smiled. She liked Simone.

"Well, we will leave you two to it," Lucy said. "I will regroup with you all when I am back from helping my assigned child, Eloise. Gracie, come on now, Dearie." Lucy took Gracie's hand and they walked back to the Kystra.

• •

"Where are we going?" Gracie asked.

"A bit more of a history lesson before I'm off."

Lucy and Gracie arrived at the Elklis, below the main floor of Norizon, down a winding stone staircase. It was a perfectly square room with framed pictures hanging on the walls, side by side in dozens and dozens of rows. The rows went up so high, you couldn't see the top.

"These are all those who are lost from Norizon," Lucy said quietly, motioning to the images of Keepers.

"These were good Keepers, with good intentions. They lived lives and helped others in theirs. But when a child loses that sparkle, all is lost…But we keep going, because that is what we do."

Gracie exhaled, and you could see her breath. The air was cold in the Elklis.

"Don't lose your sparkle, Gracie, no matter what happens. That sparkle may make a huge difference if you are able to shine it on a child with a broken dream before you become separated. Understand me now, child?" Lucy ended her question very sternly.

Gracie nodded and shivered at the same time.

"How about you keep my jacket for tonight to keep warm, hmm?" Lucy took off her large brown trench coat with its yellow belt and put it around Gracie's shoulders.

It was just the next day when Gracie stood in the same spot in the Elklis, staring at the newest picture being hung by Helfi—that of Grandma Lucy, who had gone missing

• •

in Eloise's broken dream the night before. In that picture, Lucy looked so heroic. As she stared at her grandmother, Gracie tightened the belt on the jacket her grandmother had left her in.

Helfi walked past Gracie to return to his middle console and hand out assignments to Keepers. He patted her on the back.

Gracie turned to walk back up the winding staircase, and each burning torch that she passed went out behind her.

"So much for sparkle," Gracie said as she climbed the stairs, trying to not let the tears fall.

Fast Forward to Gracie and Bernice in Perna

A figure appeared in the distance, moving slowly toward us.

The laughter that only Fefe and Bernice had heard before now became apparent to me and the Fefettes. The sound gave us all goosebumps.

I clenched the yellow belt around my waist. I hadn't taken off Grandma Lucy's jacket since losing her. Wearing it made me feel like she was with me on each of my cases. It was my "sparkle."

The laughter sounded like it was getting closer, and as we waved away a cloud of glitter in front of us, we saw her.

• •

9

Chapitre Neuf...

Before our eyes stood a woman with sparkly Black skin, wearing a red-feathered long dress. She had a wide mouth that displayed almost all of her teeth, and she exuded warmth and joy, except she seemed to be annoyed.

"It's the woman I saw! The woman who's the statue!" Bernice shouted and grabbed my arm.

"You girl," the woman pointed to Fefe, "have created quite the mess, quite the mess indeed."

Fefe looked behind her to her Fefettes, who tiptoed back while humming and then faded away with the sound of a swoosh.

The waves of shimmering green and silver lights in the sky above us went dim, stars flickered into view, and the white ground started to sparkle as Pearl began to speak.

"I appear here on this eve, before The Witching Hour, to enlighten you." She looked at me and then Bernice, and then her eyes went back to Fefe.

"What's The Witching Hour? And Pearl, what happened to you? I thought you had transitioned into Kenos, your next phase, and now watched over us all?" Fefe came closer to Pearl, who had a glowing aura.

Pearl waved her hand. "Oh, that was something I did, to temporarily have me frozen in time, so I could step back and let you all realize you didn't need me. You needed no one but yourselves."

Fefe looked confused, eagerly wanting answers from Pearl. The guards standing entry at the chimneys leading to all the other dream worlds didn't move.

"And The Witching Hour was what I called my performance every night. It was the curse that opened its door to me, and I walked right in blindly."

We all sat and listened as Pearl told us her tale.

Flashback to a Younger Pearl in Perna

Pearl sat amongst the green puddles of grass and glistening surfaces of solid water in Perna. A firefly appeared in front of her and flickered with gold dust. The swaying, sparkling willow added to the shimmer surrounding Pearl. She sensed something coming. She didn't know what it was but had the feeling that it was something good.

Pearl thought she heard a crack in the distance, but when she looked behind her she saw only the little wooden houses of Perna floating in their grass puddles.

• •

She focused her attention back to the sky, where the stars were glowing above her and her firefly friend circulated around her. She hummed to herself and dreamed of all the things she wanted to do.

A quake of Perna interrupted her daydream.

"What was that?" Pearl asked the firefly.

The firefly said nothing, and Pearl became startled at the number of fireflies that started to appear around her. "Oh, what a marvel," she thought to herself.

A wave of fireflies began to swirl around Pearl. She felt that this was an important moment. Felt like a door had opened to a home she never knew existed.

She started to sing.

Meanwhile, the quakes had worried the residents of Perna. They had never felt the trembles before. Some seemed to have been waking from a slumber.

Great cracking sounds could be heard.

Pearl, who was distracted by the wave of fireflies, was lost in her song and the dreams she was thinking of.

"Oh, this is marvelous," she thought. She sang and twirled as the light of the fireflies began to intensify.

Bishop, a blustery character who liked to put themselves in charge, was trying to gather the residents together.

"Follow me, all of you, we must go to the cracks! It's time to push through."

"Push through what?" a follower asked.

"The noise! Why, what a distraction it is. We must push through it in order for it to stop."

At that moment, Pearl was twirling, oblivious to the building chaos in Perna. Thoughts of nothing but her desires filled her head. And then, *she* appeared...Grelda.

"Where are you going? And what do you wish?" Grelda asked Pearl, in her calm, smooth voice.

"Going?" Pearl asked, startled by Grelda's presence.

"Why, everyone's going somewhere. Where is it you wish to go? Somewhere else, or over there?" Grelda pointed to the glowing weeping willow that was still swaying in the air.

"I wish to go and perform. Oh, I am so meant to be under lights and entertaining a crowd!"

"You may have all the entertaining you want," Grelda said matter of factly.

"Really?" Pearl was eager. But, she thought, "There has to be a catch, right? What's the catch?"

"You may have everything you ever wanted," Grelda purred, "as long as you stay in this world. The others will be your constant admirers and your nightly audience. So long as you sing at this time tomorrow night, and every night after that, your voice will give this place its purpose, and therefore its gift. The sound will keep everyone in place, applauding you, forever."

Pearl could think of nothing more delightful and agreed on the spot to the deal with Grelda.

Fast Forward to Pearl Telling Her Story to Fefe, Gracie and Bernice

"And so I did. I sang every night and everyone stayed here. A curse was born and I never realized it until many, many nights later. You see, I was never meant to stay here. Nor were you," Pearl pointed to Fefe. "We were meant to spread through her." Her head motioned to Bernice.

"Me?" Bernice asked.

"Why yes, of course. Haven't you felt it? That tingling inside of you, that curiosity you wake up with each day? Wanting to explore…your life?"

Bernice looked at me. I looked at Pearl.

"This isn't a dream world, girl," Pearl sighed, trying to explain to me what she thought should have been obvious to a Keeper. (Clearly, I still had a lot to learn.) "I am Inspiration. Her inspiration." She looked at Bernice. "I felt it that night long ago, when I first became inspired, reached that time of wonderment. But I became lost in my own wonder, and kept everyone here. And by the way, those fireflies? And everyone else here? Why, they are sparks."

"Sparks?" I asked.

"The sparks of inspiration that cause humans to dream, and wonder…and seek. My deal with Grelda was a curse that left us here. And I realized it when I followed the crack after another tiresome encore of singing. I knew it would only be fixed by my disappearing and giving the sparks a chance to do what they were meant to do. Grow. A statue I

• •

became, and upon my exit another deal was made, keeping the curse in place."

Pearl looked at Fefe and shook her head. "Another deal was mistaken."

"I didn't know!" Fefe cried, sinking into the ground and throwing her head in her lap.

"Sheesh, Grelda sure isn't the most sophisticated witch, is she?" I said aloud to the group.

"Well she is in charge of every child's dream universe. She can't help but to lose track of what's happening sometimes. Her intentions were good: to fulfill a wish. But…she slipped into the wrong place, thinking it was a dream world when she heard my desires. Really, it was Bernice who was having an awakening. That is why we are here at the dream depot. To be the inspiration to each dream world."

Everything made sense in that moment and I knew what needed to be done. Grelda needed to come fix this.

I grabbed Pearl and Fefe's hands and gestured to Bernice to do the same. With all of us in a circle holding hands, I wished for Grelda to appear. She normally feels the pull of desire, but this was urgent and I knew the joint wish would pull her there sooner.

And within seconds, there she was. Grelda's flowy purple dress and bright cape reached the ground so we couldn't see her feet. (You see, witches are rumored to have roots for feet. They draw their magic from nature and so are reluctant to show them in front of anyone.)

• •

"Now, what do you need, Gracie? I am busy making moonlight." Grelda knew me, as she taught school in Norizon dream headquarters. She taught all of us Keepers, when we were younger, how to guide children through their dream worlds and, more importantly, how to survive.

"Well, we aren't in a dream world and it seems that we have all gotten stuck in Bernice's inspiration because of a spell you cast!" I blurted out.

Grelda looked around, and suddenly noticed the glowing chimneys and realized we were in the dream depot.

"Oh my!" she said. "It seems inspiration got the best of me." Grelda looked to Pearl and Fefe.

"But you were both wondrous, Dearies."

Pearl let out a sigh of relief and looked to Fefe. "Being seen isn't everything. It was glorious, but...the feeling I had in the middle of those fireflies on that night. Nothing beats that. Not the crowds cheering or the encores. It's the sensation of awakening to inspiration."

"And nothing ever will beat that, for any child," Grelda said. "Let's fix this, right now!"

Grelda raised her wand, and shot Bernice a wink and a smile.

Sparks flew from the wand toward the glowing crack in the distance — the same crack we had passed through from Perna into the dream depot.

The sparks hit the crack, which created more cracks, cracking over all of Perna like it was an eggshell. There was

• •

an explosion and then…

Fireflies everywhere. And sparks.

The residents of Perna became sparks that flew past all of us. We could hear their conversations as they hurried by, on their way to Bernice's dream worlds.

"Oh, what it would be to dance."

"What if I went to see for myself?"

"I want someone to love."

"I want to tell a story that people want to hear."

The sparks of desire disappeared into the countless number of chimneys. All that remained of Perna was the glowing willow.

We looked at Fefe and Pearl. They too were starting to sparkle. They looked at each other and in unison said, "I want to sing." They shot by like the others into the same chimney top that was nearby.

Grelda sighed, satisfied. "My work here is done. I must get on now. I have some broken dreams to find." She looked at me just then, like she had forgotten for a moment about Grandma Lucy.

"I'm sorry, Heart," she said. She called all of her former students "Heart."

Since Grandma Lucy had become lost in the broken dream of Eloise, we had learned that broken dreams adapt into a shadow of the child. The shadow attaches itself to them, and with each broken dream the child has, the shadow becomes darker and creates a force that lingers. It is believed that is what creates a sad or angry or unhappy person. Keepers become stuck in the shadows of those children, and if you look closely, sometimes you can see two little purple eyes in them. Grandma Lucy was trapped in the little girl Eloise's shadow. We just haven't figured out how to rescue them from the dark yet.

"We will find her," Grelda said to me. With the same breath she faded away, and so did her finger that was lifting up my chin.

I stared at the glowing weeping willow tree that remained, and I felt kindred with it.

I shook myself out of it.

· ·

"Well, Bernice. It is now time for you to wake up, and from the looks of it, to be inspired."

The sky became bright gold and glitter filled the air. We heard the sound of a piano playing "Clair de Lune."

Bernice looked at me, her eyes softening into a smile.

10

Chapitre Dix...

Singing woke Bernice. She lay in a cloud of pillows, her book on top of her.

For a moment she had forgotten where she was, and the singing reminded her of her mother at home in New Orleans. But she was in New York. She could hear the sounds of cars honking.

"...Tell me, darling / I'm the only one that you love / Life could be a dream, sweetheart."

Auntie Taflinda sang, beautifully, the popular song

"Sh-Boom" that had come out that year.

Bernice sat up in bed. She felt completely rested and eager to start her first full day in New York City.

"I can't wait to see Jamay," she thought.

She hopped out of bed and put on the purple robe she'd laid onto the chair the night before, amidst piles of books.

Bernice opened her bedroom door and expected to smell breakfast. After all, having breakfast made for her every day was part of the spoiled life she had become accustomed to with her mother. But to her dismay, there was no smell of pancakes and bacon and eggs.

She brushed her teeth, wondering what she was supposed to eat. Did the aunties expect her to starve?

She walked down the hallway to confront her two aunties, who were talking and laughing in the kitchen.

"Do they not serve breakfast in New York City?!"

Sarafina was putting a croissant to her mouth to take a bite and blinked at Bernice's question.

Taflinda swatted Bernice lightly on her head with the day's newspaper. "Don't be so preposterous, Bernice. Of course we have breakfast, we are just too busy to cook it. Do you think all women wake up to serve hungry mouths like yours?"

Bernice felt silly and spoiled. "No, probably not."

Sarafina motioned for her to sit at the table and help herself to the pink box full of bakery goods.

Her aunties were already dressed for the day to go to

their respective jobs.

"Going to do any movie stars' hair today, Auntie Sarafina?"

"Hmmmm, well I have a strict confidentiality policy with my clientele, so the crazy men with the cameras don't show up." Sarafina leaned down to whisper to Bernice, "Elizabeth Taylor will be gracing us with her presence today."

Bernice's eyes widened as she took a big bite out of a croissant. She had dipped it into a plate of butter on the table. She was not used to breakfast being so loosey-goosey, but she embraced it. The croissant was delicious. She took such a big bite that it filled her whole mouth and flakes spilled out.

"Now, I'm sure that you are so famished that you couldn't wait to take more bites," Taflinda said, standing at the counter and sipping her coffee.

"I'm just so hungry from all the walking I did yesterday," Bernice defended herself, taking another mouthful of croissant.

"To enjoy an appetite, that's all a gal can hope for," Taflinda said, closing the newspaper and taking a last sip of her coffee. "Have to finish getting gussied up for work. Bernice dear, go get ready. Jamay will be here before long and you mustn't keep her waiting."

"I'm heading to work, Taflinda, b'bye," Sarafina called after her. She moved to the foyer and looked at the pile of hats on the table nearby. Which one to wear atop her tall hair? She tried on a few that didn't fit quite right, then gave up, hatless.

• •

"Always remember, Bernice, you don't have to put Christmas ornaments on everything. Not everything needs to be dressed up. But one must try at least to see the different looks. It's called contrast."

Sarafina opened the apartment door and sashayed out of it. "Have a great day, Bernice. Toodles, poodles."

"Contrast," Bernice thought as she walked to her bedroom to get dressed. "What will be the contrast of today from yesterday?" She looked for a casual dress for Day Two in the city.

She wanted to look good for Jamay, who dressed so colorfully and was so much fun. She looked at herself in the mirror standing in the corner of her room. The new dress her mother packed for her was sufficient. It was ivory, with a collared top and cuffed arms and a ruffled knee-length skirt, black trim and a belt. But it needed something. Her gaze went to the top right corner of the mirror, and there lay a blue ribbon that tied some of the books her aunties had gotten her. I was sitting on a pile of books, watching Bernice. I was impressed by her fashion sense.

Bernice finished tying the shiny ribbon in her black hair, creating a band. She looked in the mirror and seemed satisfied.

"Knock knock! Taf, you home? Bern, you here?" Jamay invited herself in. She walked into the kitchen and started to pick at the box of baked goodies on the table.

"I'm still dressing," Taflinda shouted from her bedroom. "Bernice, Jamay is here. Have fun now."

• •

Bernice opened her door and pranced down the hallway, feeling her dress swish with her.

"Mornin' Bern. Ready for Day Two?" Jamay licked her fingers.

"Yep, I am ready to see what today brings."

"Well...let me tell ya', it's gonna bring a lot. And ya' know why?" Jamay started talking in a heavy New York accent, which she loved to mimic.

Bernice shook her head.

"Because ya' gorgeous...and it's not just that ya' gorgeous, but that ya' good." Jamay motioned for Bernice to follow her down the hall and out the door.

Bernice smiled as she walked past the pile of hats by the door. Her Auntie Sarafina tried them on every day, but never chose one to wear. That was her routine, and she didn't feel fully dressed unless she'd tried every hat.

Down the elevator and out to the lobby Bernice and Jamay went. They walked past Lonnie the doorman, who was filling in a resident with the latest gossip.

Walking out of The Apthorp, Bernice waited while Jamay went to the curb to hail a taxi. She saw Louis and Dalton turning the corner and walking toward the entrance of the building.

They were laughing. Louis was clearly saying something that Dalton found funny. Dalton touched Louis' hand briefly. She smiled and waved, and they waved back.

· ·

"Bernice! Let's go, chica! Cabs don't wait foreva' around here." Jamay really had that New York accent down.

In the cab, the windows were down. The summer air called for it. The radio blared a song by Frank Sinatra. *"...Let me see what spring is like on Jupiter and Mars..."*

Bernice scooted closer to the open window in the taxi and poked her head out.

"This summer will be the best ever," she thought. She wondered what would happen as she explored New York City. Wondered who she'd meet, wondered what she'd do. She felt tingly and curious, sparking with excitement for it all. Then she thought of a dream she'd had, of a singer and a statue and the wonder of Pearl.

• •

ABOUT THE

ABOUT THE
Author

Brandt Ricca is a D.C.-based entrepreneur. Having a writing background and a family history of owning a newspaper, telling stories has always been at the forefront of Brandt's mindset.

Creating a narrative is a must for Brandt, who always wants to convey a message with events or imagery through his branding agency, Nora Lee by Brandt Ricca.

Brandt was born in Baton Rouge, Louisiana, and loves the Southern culture and creative atmosphere of New Orleans, which inspired the setting for the life of Barris Hart.

illustrator

Matt Miller is a designer and artist that bounces back and forth from D.C. and Florida. For as long as he can remember, Matt has had a passion for expressing his ideas and creativity in drawings and paintings. His artistic background and love for interior design and architecture are the foundation for his interior design and rendering business, Perspective.

With a soft spot for historic architecture of the American South, and gathering inspiration from his own vivid dreams, he felt he was the perfect fit for illustrating the world of the Barris Books series.

www.ingramcontent.com/pod-product-compliance
Lightning Source LLC
Chambersburg PA
CBHW040828120726
48005CB00012B/1542